ON HERMAN'S POND

Written and illustrated by
Nancy Karre

Layout, design and editing by
Andrew Karre

A Battle Creek Area Mathematics and Science Center Book
Copyright 2004 Nancy Karre

Luke the Lizard went down to the pond to play.
The water felt cool on a hot, sunny day.

Luke ran through the tall grass to the water's edge,
Where he found his friends sunning on a rocky ledge.

There was Tuck the turtle and Freda the frog
And his best friend Herman, sitting on a log.

Luke scooped up some water in his two front feet.
"Ah," he sighed, "this clear water is a cooling treat."

Luke slid into the water to join his friend the snail.
He moved through the water using his feet and tail.

"Hello Luke!" Herman greeted him with a smile.
"Jump on the log, and sit with me for a while."

"The water is cool," laughed Luke. "The water is clear.
So jump off your log and join me in here."

The snail laughed and slid into the water with the lizard.
They splashed and swam both forward and backward.

"The water looks clear and pure," said Luke. "I'm glad!"
"It is not pure water," said a voice from a nearby lilypad.

Luke and Herman turned to see who was talking.
It was a grandfather turtle sitting on a lilypad, rocking.

The turtle went on, "Pure water is clear; that is true,
But it has no taste for me and you."

Herman tasted the water with a tiny sip.
"Tastes like weeds and dirt," he said, licking his lips.

"Pond water has an odor that you can smell, too.
Take a sniff," said the turtle. "You will find it is true."

Luke closed his eyes and took a sniff through his nose.
"This water," he said, "smells like something that grows."

Herman and Luke put their heads under the surface.
They opened their eyes to see tiny specks come into focus.

"I see things!" called Herman as his head came to the top.
"Me too!" agreed Luke. "The water has many tiny spots."

"Pure water," said Luke, "has no taste for you and me."
"No odor to smell," agreed Herman, "or color to see."

"Hooray!" cried the turtle. "You learn quite fast.
Now you can learn about water as liquid, solid, or gas!"

The old turtle picked a lilypad
And folded it into a square-shaped doodad.

"Fill the container with water," he said.
"Then tell me what shape comes into your head."

Herman and Luke did as they were told,
And filled the lilypad box with all it could hold.

"The water," said Luke, "takes on the shape of the square.
It moves to the sides of the box, here and there."

"That's right!" said the old turtle, "Now watch me.
I'll change the shape of the container, look and see."

Turtle unfolded the large lilypad,
And folded it again until Luke knew what he had.

"It's a triangle!" declared the young lizard.
"You fold shapes like a storybook wizard."

The turtle laughed and gave the triangle to the snail.
Herman filled it with water and smiled at the three-sided pail.

"Liquid water needs a boundary to form a shape.
The sides will not allow the water to escape."

"Liquid water will move to fit the shape of the holder,
But what happens to water when it becomes much colder?"

"Luke and Herman, you have listened well.
Now let us learn about water as hard as my shell."

"When the temperature of water gets very cold,
Water freezes and becomes something you can hold."

"When water freezes, it becomes hard, cold ice,
Or snowflakes that fall to make a white paradise."

"Last winter," said Herman, "we had ice and snow.
The water did change, that much we know."

"Think about winter when the air is cold.
The pond is frozen and has pieces you can hold."

"When water gets cold, below 32 degrees,
The liquid water changes and begins to freeze."

"Each piece of ice or each tiny snowflake
Has its own shape, make no mistake."

"The shape of ice will not be changed,
No matter how often the box is rearranged."

Luke and Herman dreamed of cold weather
And how much fun they would have playing together.

The pond would be fun for slipping and sliding,
And snow forts would be made for running and hiding.

"When the temperature of ice gets quite warm,
Solid ice will melt and change to its liquid form."

"One lesson is missing in your water education:
When water changes to gas, it is called evaporation!"

"As the summer gets hotter, our pond will shrink.
There will be a little less water for us to drink."

"Tiny droplets will move into warmer air,
Ever so slowly; we will not be aware."

"Look very closely at the water's edge.
Do you see the water marks on the rocky ledge?"

"Where does the water go?" asked Luke with concern.
"I'm not sure I wish to learn."

"Don't be alarmed," said the turtle. "You will see,
The water returns as rain eventually."

"When the air temperature cools down a bit,
Clouds of rain droplets form, and a shower will hit."

"I am so happy," said Herman, "for the rain showers.
I could swim in our pond for hours and hours."

"Come for a swim, Turtle. The water is grand."
"I will," he replied. "I like water so much better than land!"

Water Works - Exploring Like a Scientist!

Water is natural child's play for children of all ages. The simple act of playing with toys and containers in the bathtub, pool, or sink helps children in their skills and understanding of volume, pouring, measuring, describing, questioning, as well as the properties of liquid water. Transform a few common materials into a young scientist's "Water Works" laboratory.

DOES THE SHAPE AND SIZE OF CONTAINERS MAKE A DIFFERENCE IN HOW FAST WATER EVAPORATES?

What you need:
    a variety of containers: cups, bowls, narrow containers, wide containers, etc. Be sure all the containers can hold at least 1/2 cup of water.
    measuring cup
    water
    clock
    paper and pencil for recording your results
    crayon or marker to mark the water level

What you do:
1. Pour 1/2 cup of water into each container you have selected.
2. Mark the water level on each container.
3. Make a chart and record the time you began your experiment.
4. Leave your containers out on the counter or table over night and check the water level the next day.
5. Look at the water level for each container. Did it change?
6. Pour the water from the first container into the measuring cup. Record the amount of water left in the container.
7. Pour the water back into the container after your have recorded your measurement. Be careful not to spill!
8. Repeat steps 6 & 7 with the rest of the containers.
9. Leave your containers out for one more night and repeat the measurement the next day.

What you talk about:
Ask your child to explain the results of the experiment. Tell your child that the water in the wide containers evaporate into the air faster than the water in the narrow containers because wider containers let more water come in contact with the air. Narrow containers have more water below the surface and less water in contact with the air.

About the author:

Nancy Karre was born in Flint, Michigan. She graduated from the University of Wyoming with a Bachelor of Science Degree. She moved to Battle Creek, Michigan in 1977 with her husband, Nelson. They have three sons and one daughter. Nancy began writing children's science literature in 1996 and currently writes science activities and literature for the Battle Creek Area Mathematics and Science Center K-6 Outreach Program.

About the Battle Creek Area Mathematics and Science Center:

The Battle Creek Area Mathematics and Science Center was established in 1990. The Battle Creek Area Mathematics and Science Center delivers educational services in mathematics, science, and technology to area students, teachers, and administrators. Its mission is to foster improved mathematics, science and technology instruction to all students in grades K-12, provide accelerated enrichment instruction to area students in grades 9-12, provide quality professional staff development for area K-12 educators, and build lasting partnerships with area businesses and industries. The Battle Creek Area Mathematics and Science Center develops classroom science kits for grades K-6 based on the State and National Science Education Standards.